Rihanna
the Seahorse
Fairy

by Daisy Meadows

ORCHARD

The Fairyland Palace

Barn

Farmhouse

Stables

Clubhouse

CAMP

Adventure Lake

Birdwatching Tower

There are seven special animals,
Who live in Fairyland.
They use their magic powers
To help others where they can.

A dragon, black cat, firebird,
A seahorse and snow swan too,
A unicorn and ice bear -
I know just what to do.

I'll lock them in my castle
And never let them out.
The world will turn more miserable,
Of that, I have no doubt...

Contents

Adventure Lake

"Oh, I'm really looking forward to going canoeing again!" Kirsty Tate said eagerly to her best friend, Rachel Walker. The girls were carrying a lightweight canoe on their shoulders as they walked through the camp towards Adventure Lake. "But I'm going to try to keep my feet dry this time!"

Rachel laughed. "Yes, it's good fun, isn't it?" she agreed. "I'm glad we've got some free time this afternoon so that we can have another go."

"We're not just here to have fun though, are we?" Kirsty added, glancing around to check that none of the other campers were close enough to hear. "We're trying to help our fairy friends, too!"

On the day the girls arrived at the adventure camp, the King and Queen of Fairyland had asked for their help to find seven missing Magical Animals.

These special young animals had
amazing powers that helped to spread
the kind
of magic that humans as well as fairies
could possess – the wonderful gifts of
imagination, good luck, humour,
friendship, compassion, healing
and courage.

The seven Magical
Animal Fairies
spent a whole year
training these
youngsters before
they returned to
their families in
Fairyland, ready
to use their special
talents to help everyone
in both the human and the fairy worlds.

However, spiteful Jack Frost was
determined to put a stop to all this,

simply because he
wanted everyone
to be as lonely
and miserable
as him. So he
and his naughty
goblin servants
had kidnapped the
Magical Animals and
taken them to his Ice Castle. But the
animals had managed to escape, and
now they had hidden themselves away
in the human world. Rachel and Kirsty
were determined to find all seven
Magical Animals before Jack Frost and
his goblins did, and then return them
safely to Fairyland.

"We've done quite well so far, haven't we, Kirsty?" Rachel remarked. "We've found Ashley's dragon, Lara's black cat and Erin's firebird."

Kirsty nodded. "I just hope we find the others before the end of the week—" she began. But just then Lorna, one of the camp counsellors, came out of a nearby tent, and Kirsty and Rachel exchanged a warning glance. Both girls knew that *no one* in the human world could ever find out about the existence of fairies.

"Ah, I see you're off to Adventure Lake, girls," Lorna remarked with a smile. "Don't forget to put your life jackets on, will you? And if you need any help, there are always lots of counsellors around the lake."

"OK, Lorna," Kirsty replied. "We'll be careful."

"Well, the secret to fun and successful canoeing is teamwork," Lorna said, with a twinkle in her eye. "So you two should be brilliant at it because you're such good friends!"

Kirsty and Rachel grinned at each other as Lorna went off.

"Not just good friends," Rachel laughed. "*Best* friends!"

Adventure Lake lay at the edge of the camp, the surface of the water rippling and shimmering in the sunlight. Carefully, Rachel and Kirsty laid the canoe down at the water's edge and began to put on their life jackets. As they did so, Catherine, one of their room-mates, came running up to them.

"Hi, you two!" she cried, smiling happily. "Guess what? I just passed my swimming test!"

"Well done!" Kirsty said warmly.

"That's great, Catherine," Rachel agreed. "What are you doing for the rest of free time? Do you want to ride in the canoe with us?"

Catherine shook her head. "Thanks, but I'm going swimming with Emma, Natasha and Katie," she replied. "Now that I've passed my test, I'm allowed to swim out to the end of the floating dock." She pointed at the wooden dock that led from the shore and out across the lake. The rest of their room-mates were already splashing around there and shrieking with laughter.

"Are you two coming to craft time later?" Catherine went on. "I think we're making friendship bracelets."

"We definitely won't miss that!" Kirsty laughed. "We want to make friendship bracelets for you and all the other girls in our cabin."

"I think you'll both get lots of bracelets back in return!" Catherine said with a grin. "Have a good time canoeing. By the way" – she winked at Rachel and Kirsty – "you'd better watch out for the mythical creature that lives at the bottom of the lake!"

Rachel and Kirsty glanced at each other in shock.

What mythical creature did Catherine mean? Kirsty thought, confused. Could it be one of the Magical Animals she and Rachel were searching for? And how did Catherine know? Everything about Fairyland was supposed to be a secret!

Catherine laughed. "Don't look so serious, you two!" she teased. "The lake creature is just an old legend, that's all. See you later!" And she ran off.

"Phew, I was worried there for a minute!" Rachel whispered to Kirsty, looking relieved as they clambered into the canoe.

"Me, too!" Kirsty replied, settling herself into the front seat. "Ready, Rachel?"

They pushed themselves away from the bank with their paddles, and then set off across the water, rowing smoothly and rhythmically. The girls could see bright-blue dragonflies skimming across the surface of the lake, and there were lots of ducks quacking loudly, and occasionally dipping their heads underwater.

As Rachel and Kirsty passed by the floating dock, they waved at their friends and then paddled on.

"There are lots of campers enjoying the water today," Rachel remarked, spotting several other girls in boats, canoes and kayaks. "Shall we row across to the other bank, Kirsty?"

Kirsty nodded. When they eventually approached the opposite bank, she noticed a crescent-shaped cove among the rocks.

"Look, Rachel!" Kirsty pointed at the entrance to the cove. "Shall we explore it?"

"OK," Rachel agreed, "But don't forget we have to be back at camp for craft time."

"Oh, we've got plenty of time," Kirsty replied.

The girls rowed up to the entrance of the cove and peered inside.

"I can hear splashing," Rachel said, her eyes wide with excitement. "Let's follow the cove all the way round, Kirsty – that splashing noise might be a waterfall!"

Kirsty shook her head.

"I've changed my mind," she said with a shrug. "The cove's OK, but I want to row around the rest of the lake."

"That's *boring!*" Rachel complained. "I want to explore the cove!"

"No way!" Kirsty snapped, turning round to glare at Rachel.

"Why should we do what *you* want?" Rachel retorted crossly.

Suddenly the girls stared at each other in shock. They had never, ever argued before!

"Sorry, Rachel," Kirsty blurted out. "I don't know what came over me!"

"I'm sorry too!" Rachel gasped, looking very ashamed. Both girls put their paddles down and hugged each other.

"That was horrible – I never want to argue with you again, Kirsty!"

"Me neither," Kirsty agreed. "Look, we've just got time to explore the cove *and* the rest of the lake."

"Good idea," Rachel agreed.

Swiftly the girls paddled along the crescent of the cove. As they rounded the curve, Kirsty spotted another canoe just ahead of them. She frowned as she stared at the little boat. The three passengers looked very familiar!

"Rachel!" Kirsty whispered urgently. "Goblins!"

Goblin Fishermen

Rachel peeped over Kirsty's shoulder, and her heart sank when she saw three goblins sitting in the canoe. They were holding a large fishing net.

"They must think one of the Magical Animals is hiding in the lake!" Kirsty whispered.

"Quick, we mustn't let them see us!"

Rachel replied in a low voice.

The girls paddled swiftly and silently towards a nearby inlet. They moored the canoe safely and then slipped down inside it, out of sight.

"I wonder which of the Magical Animals is in the lake?" Rachel murmured, as they peered carefully over the edge of the canoe.

The goblins were each holding a corner of the net, ready to fling it into the water.

"NOW!" shouted the biggest goblin.

The goblins tried to toss the net into
the water, but instead the breeze blew it
back at them, and they all got tangled
up. The goblins shrieked with fury as the
boat rocked violently from side to side.

"Help!" shouted the smallest goblin as
he almost went overboard. He flung out
his arms, trying to steady himself,
and hit the biggest
goblin square
on the nose.

"I'll get you
for that!" the
biggest goblin
yelled, lunging at
him. But his foot
caught in the net and he pitched
forward, head-butting the third goblin
in the tummy.

"Ow, that hurt!" the third goblin roared angrily.

The three goblins glared at each other, clenching their fists. But then, to Kirsty and Rachel's surprise, the smallest goblin stepped forward, smiling apologetically.

"Please forgive me," he said politely. "That was all *my* fault."

"No, no," the biggest goblin interrupted quickly, "*I* was to blame."

"Ah, time for a group hug!" said the third goblin. And, to Rachel and Kirsty's astonishment, the goblins huddled together and put their arms lovingly around one another!

"This is weird!" Rachel whispered. "Why are the goblins being so nice to each other?"

"I don't know," Kirsty replied, as the goblins gathered up the net again and threw it into the water. "Let's keep watching!"

The goblins waited a moment and then began pulling the net in again.

"We've caught something!" the biggest goblin shrieked triumphantly. He pulled a wriggling silver fish from the net and held it up. "Is this a seahorse?"

"No, but well done, anyway!" the smallest goblin said kindly.

The big goblin threw the fish back into
the lake. Then he rummaged in the net
again and held up an old, battered boot.

"Well, is *this* a seahorse?"

The other goblins shook their heads.
"No seahorses here!" they chorused,
peering down at the net.

Rachel frowned, looking confused.
"Kirsty, seahorses don't live in lakes,"
she whispered. "They're only found in
the sea."

"The goblins must be looking for Rihanna's Magic Seahorse!" Kirsty pointed out excitedly. "A magic seahorse would be able to live *anywhere!*"

"Oh, of course!" Rachel gasped. "The Magic Seahorse's special power is the gift of friendship. That must be why the goblins are being so nice to each other!"

"And remember that the young animals aren't always in control of their magical powers because they're still being trained," Kirsty reminded her.

"Their magic can sometimes work in reverse – and that must be why we squabbled with each other just now!"

"So the Magic Seahorse is definitely around here somewhere!" Rachel exclaimed.

Suddenly the girls' canoe began to rock slightly from side to side.

"What's happening?" Kirsty whispered.

She and Rachel peeked over the edge of the canoe. To their

amazement, the water around them was filled with sparkling, rainbow-coloured bubbles that were causing their canoe to sway gently.

"It's magic!" Rachel gasped, as the bubbles swirled around them. "Do you think there really *is* a mythical creature in the lake?"

"Or maybe it's the Magic Seahorse!" Kirsty suggested. "But how are we going to find him before the goblins do? We don't have a fishing net!"

Suddenly a stream of bubbles shot up into the air. A second later, a tiny fairy burst from the water with a shimmering splash, and hovered in the air above Rachel and Kirsty!

Underwater Magic

"Hello, Kirsty and Rachel!" the fairy called, casting a wary glance at the goblins as she floated down towards the girls' canoe. She had long blonde hair in flowing waves, and she wore a floaty sea-green kaftan with a beaded hem. "I'm Rihanna the Seahorse Fairy!"

"Oh, Rihanna, it's great to see you!"

Kirsty cried with a huge smile. "We think your Magic Seahorse is right here in this lake!"

"But we're not sure how to find him," Rachel added. She pointed at the other canoe. "The goblins are after him, too!"

Rihanna nodded. "You're right, girls," she agreed. "My darling Bubbles is definitely around here somewhere. I can *feel* it! Will you help me find him?"

"Of course we will," Kirsty said eagerly, "but how—?"

Their discussion was interrupted by
loud yells from the goblins' canoe as they
pulled the net in again.

"This isn't working!" the smallest
goblin complained,
taking another
fish out and
tossing it
back into
the lake.

"Let's go
and search under
the water then," the big goblin suggested.

"How?" the third goblin said with a
shrug. "We can't breathe underwater!"

Rachel, Kirsty and Rihanna
watched as the big goblin bent down
and pulled something out from under
one of the seats.

37

"We can use magic to help us!" he said, waving an ice wand in the air.

The other goblins looked astonished.

"Where did you get *that*?" the smallest goblin demanded.

"Jack Frost gave it to me for emergencies," the big goblin replied. "Now that three of the Magical Animals have already been returned to Fairyland, he didn't want to take any chances!"

Rachel, Kirsty and Rihanna stared at each other in dismay.

"So why haven't we used the wand before?" asked the third goblin with a frown.

The big goblin looked rather sheepish.

"I forgot I had it," he mumbled, shuffling his feet.

The other two goblins glared at him in disgust. For a moment Kirsty thought they were going to start a fight over the wand, but then the smallest goblin shrugged.

"Let's just get on with it then," he said politely. "Agreed?"

"Agreed!" said the other two.

"My seahorse's magic is making them be nice to each other!" Rihanna whispered as the goblins began folding up the fishing-net. "Girls, we *must* find Bubbles before the goblins do. And you'll be able to swim faster if you're fairy-sized like me!"

A flick of Rihanna's wand sent a shower of fairy sparkles drifting around Rachel and

Kirsty. Immediately, they shrank until they were as small as Rihanna herself, with the same translucent wings on their backs.

"The canoe suddenly seems huge!" Rachel laughed, glancing around.

Rihanna lifted her wand again, and this time two shiny bubbles streamed through the air towards Rachel and Kirsty. The girls felt the bubbles settle over their heads, and then burst with a pop.

"Now you'll be able to breathe underwater, just like when you had your adventure with Shannon the Ocean Fairy," Rihanna reminded them. "Let's go!"

Rachel, Kirsty and Rihanna fluttered over the side of the canoe. They were just about to dive into the water when there was a shout from the goblins.

"Look! Fairies!"

Dismayed, the girls and Rihanna
glanced round. They'd been spotted!
They saw the big goblin wave the ice
wand at his friends, and goggles and
flippers magically appeared on their
heads and feet.

"Quick, girls!" Rihanna shouted.

The three friends plunged
into the waters of the lake.
It was a little chilly and
both Kirsty and Rachel
gasped as they sank
lower. Shoals of tiny fish
wove their way past the
girls, and the bottom of the
lake was carpeted with
beautiful green plants, their
leaves waving gently in the
rippling waters.

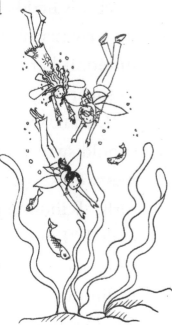

"I didn't realise there was so much going on under the surface!" Kirsty said, as a little frog swam past them.

"It's just as exciting down here as it is on land!" Rachel added. Then she laughed as a duck floating above them stuck his head underwater and stared at her in surprise.

"I think we should swim westwards, girls," Rihanna called. "I'm not sure, but I have a feeling we may find Bubbles in that direction."

"I wonder where the goblins are?"
Kirsty remarked as they followed
Rihanna to the west. "Let's hope
they've gone eastwards!"
Rachel, Kirsty and
Rihanna began to
search for the
missing seahorse
among the
plants at the
bottom of
the lake. But
it was hard
work. The
lake was huge,
and the water
was quite misty,
making it difficult
to see very far ahead.

Rachel and Kirsty both began to feel rather downhearted. How would they ever find Bubbles before the goblins did?

"Girls, I have an idea!" Rihanna announced, hovering in the water. "I have a friend who lives here in the deepest part of the lake's underwater canyon. I think he'll be able to help us find Bubbles more quickly!"

"Oh, I hope so!" Kirsty said eagerly.

Rihanna began to sing:

> *This is a special message*
> *Rihanna sends to you,*
> *We need your help,*
> *We need it fast,*
> *Please don't delay,*
> *Come straight away!*

46

"Charlie!" Rihanna called when she had finished her song. "Charlie, where are you?"

Rachel and Kirsty exchanged a confused look as the water around them began to fizz and bubble.

Who *was* this mysterious creature called Charlie?

Leggy Garden!

Suddenly, Rachel gripped Kirsty's arm.

"Look!" she cried.

A large shape, the colour of an elephant, was swimming towards them through the bubbles. The strange creature had a long neck and a humped back.

"What *is* it?" Kirsty whispered. "It looks a bit like pictures I've seen of the Loch Ness Monster!"

"Charlie!" Rihanna called, waving at the creature. "Over here!"

Charlie was smiling warmly at them as he swam closer. Rachel was very relieved, as otherwise she might have been quite scared of him. Charlie was *so* big!

"Girls, this is my dear friend Charlie," Rihanna announced with a grin. "He's lived in the lake for years. In fact, people tell stories about him, although no one's ever really seen him."

"Oh!" Rachel gasped. "Charlie must be the mythical creature that Catherine mentioned!"

Rihanna nodded, her eyes twinkling. "Charlie is actually a retired Magical Animal!" she explained. "Now he lives a nice quiet life at the bottom of Adventure Lake. Charlie, these are my friends, Rachel and Kirsty."

"Hi, Charlie," the girls chorused.

"We're searching for Bubbles, my Magic Seahorse," Rihanna went on. "We were wondering if you'd seen him?"

Charlie looked thoughtful.

"Funny you should say that!" he replied, in a booming voice. "I've overheard some of the other lake creatures talking about a new kid who's really friendly. I'll send out a message and ask if anyone's seen him today."

Rachel and Kirsty watched in fascination as Charlie began to hum a deep, low sound that created long ripples in the water. They waited. Then, after a moment, the water began to move again, but this time the ripples of sound were coming back towards them. Charlie cocked his head and listened.

"Bubbles was last seen near the middle of the lake," Charlie announced. He pursed his mouth and blew out a stream of shining bubbles. "This underwater trail will help you find him," he went on, as the bubbles floated ahead of them. "But hurry before it vanishes. My magic doesn't last long in the human world!"

"Thank you, Charlie!" Rihanna and the girls called as they zoomed off.

The three friends swam swiftly towards the centre of the lake, following Charlie's magical trail. But, to Kirsty's dismay, she could see that the bright bubbles were already fading away.

"Swim faster, girls!" Rihanna shouted.

53

Panting hard, Rachel, Kirsty and Rihanna reached the middle of the lake just as the trail finally fizzled away. But there was no sign of Bubbles anywhere.

"Bubbles is such a friendly little seahorse," Rihanna said, as a large brown trout swam lazily by. "I'm sure he'll have made lots of friends here in the lake."

She turned to the trout. "Hello, there," Rihanna called. "Have you seen a seahorse around here?"

"I just saw one heading in the direction of Leggy Garden," the trout replied helpfully. "There were some really rude green creatures heading that way as well!"

"Goblins!" Rihanna gasped.

Rachel was just about to ask where
Leggy Garden was when
a hook with some bait
attached to it plopped
down into the water
from overhead.

"As if I'm falling for
that old one!" the trout
said scornfully. "Humans
are so predictable!" And he
swam quickly away.

Kirsty glanced up and saw the bottom
of a boat above them.

"Some of the campers must be fishing,"
she said. "We'd better move away so we
don't get hooked!"

"But where's Leggy Garden?" Rihanna
asked as they swam away from the boat.

"Let's head in the direction the trout came from," Rachel suggested.

As they swam through the water, Kirsty kept looking upwards. She could see the bottoms of kayaks, canoes and boats overhead on the surface of the lake. Suddenly she laughed.

"I know exactly where Leggy Garden is!" she announced. "Follow me!"

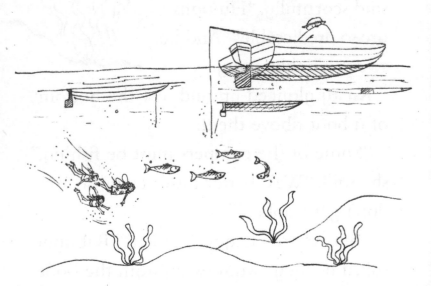

Quickly, Kirsty led Rachel and
Rihanna towards the floating dock.
Then Rachel and Rihanna burst out
laughing too. They could see the kicking
legs of some of the campers as they
swam around the dock!

"What a great name – Leggy
Garden!" Rachel remarked.

"Girls!" Rihanna exclaimed in a
dismayed voice. "I see goblins ahead!
Quick, we must make sure the swimmers
don't spot them!" And she whizzed off,
away from Leggy Garden.

Rachel and Kirsty rushed after
Rihanna towards the goblins. As they got
closer, the girls were horrified to see that
the goblins had formed a circle around a
beautiful golden seahorse.

"It's Bubbles!" Rihanna cried.

Charlie to the Rescue

Bubbles was trying to swim out of the circle of goblins. But every time he darted forward, the goblins tried to grab him, making the circle smaller as they moved in closer.

"Bubbles can't escape, and I can see he's getting tired!" Rihanna said anxiously as the little seahorse bobbed helplessly around inside the ring of goblins. "What can we do?"

Just then the big goblin glanced round and spotted them.

"Oh, hello!" he said, waving in a friendly way. "Sorry about this. We don't like to come between good friends, but we've got to do what Jack Frost says, you know!"

"Yes, it's a nasty job, but somebody has to do it!" added the smallest goblin with an apologetic smile.

"The goblins are even being nice to *us*," Kirsty whispered to Rachel.

"Bubbles' magic must be working overtime!"

"However are we going to get Bubbles back?" Rachel wondered. Then an idea unexpectedly popped into her head. "Rihanna, do you think Charlie might help us again?"

Rihanna's face lit up. "I'm sure he will!" she said eagerly. "I'll call him." And she began to sing her little song once more.

The goblins turned to stare at Rihanna, looking confused.

"What are you doing?" asked the big goblin, as the water around them began to swirl with sparkling bubbles. "This is no time for singing!"

"What's happening?" gasped the third goblin. "Why has the water gone all fizzy?"

"Well, a big old lake monster is on his way here right NOW!" Rachel said loudly. "And he won't be happy when he finds out you're trying to steal the magic seahorse. So you'd better let him go before the monster arrives!"

"Ha!" scoffed the smallest goblin. "You don't scare *us*! There's no such thing as a lake monster, and these bubbles are just a silly fairy trick!"

Laughing, he rushed forwards, breaking the circle, and this time he managed to grab Bubbles and hang onto him.

"Hurrah!" the other goblins cheered. "Group hug!"

"OK, but I can't let go of this seahorse!" the smallest goblin yelled.

As the goblins huddled together again, Charlie appeared through the mass of sparkly bubbles.

"Charlie, the goblins haven't seen you because they're too busy hugging!" Kirsty whispered. "We need to get Bubbles away from them – so can you be as scary as possible?"

With a grin, Charlie nodded. He swam silently towards the goblins, who were still noisily congratulating themselves on capturing the magic seahorse.

Then Charlie tapped the smallest goblin on the shoulder with one of his huge fins.

The Gift of Friendship

The goblins turned around.

"BOO!" Charlie yelled in a thunderous voice that sent the water around them rippling in all directions.

The goblins' eyes opened wide in horror. They screamed loudly, and the smallest goblin let go of Bubbles instantly. Then all three goblins shot off through the water, disappearing into the distance at record speed. Rachel, Kirsty and Rihanna burst out laughing.

"Charlie, you were wonderful!" Kirsty cried, and she and Rachel both gave him a big kiss on the cheek.

"Bubbles!" Rihanna called, her face shining with delight. "Here I am!"

The golden seahorse immediately bounced joyfully through the water towards her. As he did so, Bubbles began to shrink so that, by the time he jumped into Rihanna's arms, he was fairy-sized again. Rihanna gave him a hug, and Rachel and Kirsty gathered round to give him a pat, too.

"Girls, I must take Bubbles back to Fairyland," Rihanna said. "But first, let's get you back to your canoe. I think the quickest way will be to ride on Charlie's back."

"Climb aboard!" Charlie called.

Rachel and Kirsty clambered onto Charlie's grey back, and so did Rihanna, still holding Bubbles tightly. Then Charlie swam off through the water. Once again they passed underneath the boats and canoes, and through Leggy Garden.

"None of our friends would believe
that we were right below them, riding on
the back of the lake creature with a fairy
and a magic seahorse!" Kirsty whispered
to Rachel, who laughed.

Very soon they reached the canoe.

"Thank you, girls,"
Rihanna said, her
eyes sparkling.
"Because of you,
four of our
beloved Magical
Animals have now
been returned to us.
I know we can count
on you to do your best
to find the others!"

"We will," Rachel and Kirsty promised.

Rihanna smiled. "You two are very lucky because you already have the wonderful gift of friendship," she said. "But now Bubbles will be able to spread the magic of friendship even further. Goodbye!"

"Goodbye," Rachel and Kirsty called.

Rihanna pointed her wand at the girls, and a burst of fairy magic sent them shooting up out of the water in a whirlpool of glitter. A moment later they were back in their canoe, and back to human-size.

"Look, we're not even wet!" Rachel marvelled. "Isn't fairy magic wonderful!"

"I'm so glad Bubbles is safe and sound," Kirsty sighed happily.

"Me too," Rachel said. "A world without friendship would be like..." She stopped and thought for a moment.

"Fairyland without magic!" Rachel added, and Kirsty smiled and nodded in agreement.

Now it's time for Kirsty and Rachel
to help...

Sophia the Snow Swan Fairy

Read on for a sneak peek...

Kirsty Tate bit into a warm, sticky
marshmallow and smiled. Bliss! It had
been another fantastic day at the
adventure camp where she and her best
friend Rachel Walker were staying for
a week. The sun was going down and
everyone was sitting around a fire, singing
songs and toasting marshmallows. "I'm
having *such* a brilliant holiday," Kirsty
said happily to Rachel.

"Me too," Rachel agreed. Then she
lowered her voice. "Especially with our

new fairy friends!"

Kirsty smiled at her words. She and Rachel shared an amazing secret. They had met lots of fairies and had all sorts of exciting adventures with them! This week, they were helping the Magical Animal Fairies find their lost animals, after Jack Frost had stolen them. The girls had already helped the fairies find a young dragon, a magic black cat, a firebird and a seahorse…but there were still three animals left to track down and return to Fairyland.

"Listen up, guys!" came a voice just then. Kirsty and Rachel turned to see Trudi, one of the camp counsellors, standing on a tree stump. "There's such a wonderful full moon tonight, we're going to set off on a night hike. I've got something very special to show you all. Could you get into pairs, please?"

The campers immediately scrambled to pair up. Kirsty and Rachel were going together, of course, and grinned at one another. They always had their most exciting times when it was just the two of them.

Two other counsellors, Edward and Lizzy, began passing out torches.

"Why are we going hiking in the dark anyway?" a girl called Anna wanted to know...

Read Sophia the Snow Swan Fairy to find out what adventures are in store for Kirsty and Rachel!

Meet the Magical Animal Fairies

Seven magical animals are lost in the human world! Help Rachel and Kirsty reunite them with their fairy friends.

www.rainbowmagicbooks.co.uk

Meet the fairies, play games
and get sneak peeks at
the latest books!

There's fairy fun for everyone at

www.rainbowmagicbooks.co.uk

You'll find great activities, competitions, stories and
fairy profiles, and also a special newsletter.

Win Rainbow Magic Goodies!

There are lots of Rainbow Magic fairies, and we want to know which one is your favourite! Send us a picture of her and tell us in thirty words why she is your favourite and why you like Rainbow Magic books. Each month we will put the entries into a draw and select one winner to receive a Rainbow Magic Sparkly T-shirt and Goody Bag!

Send your entry on a postcard to Rainbow Magic Competition, Orchard Books, 338 Euston Road, London NW1 3BH. Australian readers should email: childrens.books@hachette.com.au New Zealand readers should write to Rainbow Magic Competition, PO Box 3255, Shortland St, Auckland 1140, NZ. Don't forget to include your name and address. Only one entry per child.

Good luck!

Meet the
Green Fairies

Jack Frost's goblins make a mess everywhere they go. Can Kirsty and Rachel clean things up before the natural world is seriously harmed?

www.rainbowmagicbooks.co.uk